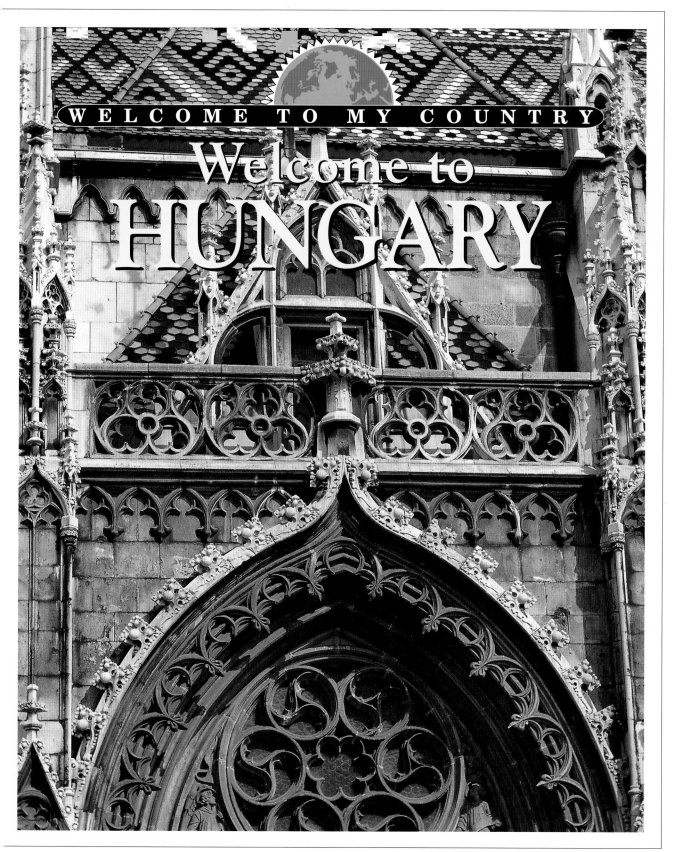

Welcome to
HUNGARY

Gareth Stevens Publishing
A WORLD ALMANAC EDUCATION GROUP COMPANY

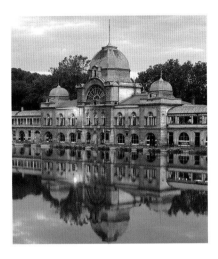

Written by
CHANG SHUH CHENG/NICOLE LUNDRIGAN

Edited in USA by
DOROTHY L. GIBBS

Designed by
GEOSLYN LIM

Picture research by
SUSAN JANE MANUEL

First published in North America in 2003 by
Gareth Stevens Publishing
A World Almanac Education Group Company
330 West Olive Street, Suite 100
Milwaukee, Wisconsin 53212 USA

Please visit our web site at:
www.garethstevens.com
For a free color catalog describing
Gareth Stevens' list of high-quality
books and multimedia programs,
call 1-800-542-2595 (USA) or
1-800-387-3178 (CANADA).
Gareth Stevens Publishing's fax: (414) 332-3567.

© **TIMES MEDIA PRIVATE LIMITED 2003**
Originated and designed by
Times Editions
An imprint of Times Media Private Limited
A member of the Times Publishing Group
Times Centre, 1 New Industrial Road
Singapore 536196
http://www.timesone.com.sg/te

Library of Congress Cataloging-in-Publication Data
Chang, Shuh Cheng.
Welcome to Hungary / Chang Shuh Cheng and Nicole Lundrigan.
p. cm. — (Welcome to my country)
Summary: An overview of the geography, history, government,
economy, people, and culture of the country that was settled by
the Magyar people in the late ninth century.
Includes bibliographical references and index.
ISBN 0-8368-2544-6 (lib. bdg.)
1. Hungary—Juvenile literature. [1. Hungary.]
I. Lundrigan, Nicole. II. Title. III. Series.
DB906.C48   2003
943.9—dc21   2002030476

Printed in Malaysia

1 2 3 4 5 6 7 8 9 07 06 05 04 03

PICTURE CREDITS
Archive Photos: 15 (all)
Art Directors and Trip Photo Library: 1, 5, 8, 25,
   30, 36, 38, 45
Sue Cunningham: 10 (top), 17, 18 (bottom),
   19, 24, 27, 32
Focus Team Photo Agency: 3 (top), 3 (bottom),
   6, 7 (both), 16 (top), 22, 23, 26, 35, 40,
   41 (top)
Getty Images/HultonArchive: 11, 12 (bottom),
   29, 31
Bridget Gubbins: 21
Blaine Harrington: cover, 16 (bottom), 41 (bottom)
The Hutchison Library: 34
MTI (Hungarian News Agency): 20, 39
Topham Picturepoint: 2, 3 (center), 4, 9 (both),
   10 (bottom), 12 (top), 13, 14, 18 (top), 28,
   33, 37

Digital Scanning by Superskill Graphics Pte Ltd

Contents

Words that appear in the glossary are printed in **boldface** type the first
time they occur in the text.

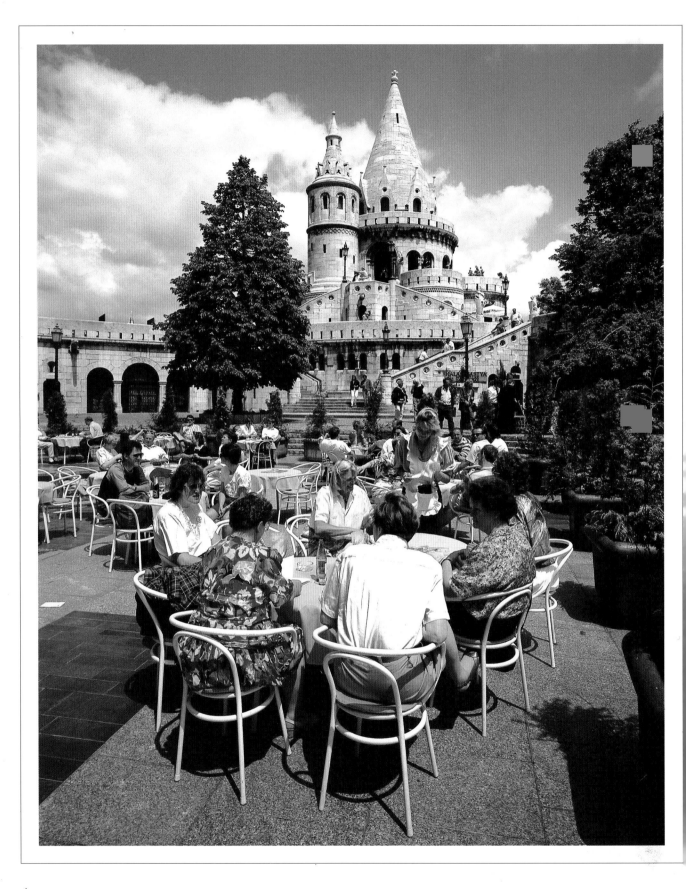

Welcome to Hungary!

Because of its central location on the continent, Hungary is often called the "crossroads of Europe." The country was established when Magyar **tribes** crossed the Carpathian Mountains, in about 896, and settled along the Danube River. Let's find out more about Hungary's history and culture.

Opposite: Although it looks like a fortress from the Middle Ages, Fisherman's Bastion, on Trinity Square in Budapest, was built between 1895 and 1902, mostly to decorate the area.

Below: Budapest is Hungary's largest city, as well as the country's capital.

The Flag of Hungary

The colors of Hungary's flag represent strength (red), faith (white), and hope (green). This flag was introduced between 1848 and 1849, during a rebellion against the ruling Hapsburg empire of Austria.

The Land

Hungary has an area of 35,919 square miles (93,030 square kilometers). It is a **landlocked** country, with Slovakia and Ukraine to the north, Romania to the east, Serbia and Croatia to the south, and Slovenia and Austria to the west. Budapest has been the country's capital since 1873. It was formed by uniting the three older cities of Buda, Óbuda, and Pest.

Below:
The Danube River divides Budapest into the hilly Buda area to the west and the flatlands of Pest to the east.

The Hungarian Plains

Most of Hungary is flat plains. An **arc** of hills, volcanic peaks, and **plateaus**, extending from the Bakony Mountains to the Northern Mountains, divides it into the Little Hungarian Plain and the Great Hungarian Plain. The Little Hungarian Plain, or Little Alföld, is northwest of the arc, while the Great Hungarian Plain, or Great Alföld, is southeast. Mount Kékes, at 3,327 feet (1,014 meters), is the highest peak.

Above: *Csikósok* (CHEE-kohsh-ohk), or Hungarian cowboys, are world famous for raising and training horses.

Climate

Like most countries in central Europe, Hungary has a temperate climate. Its somewhat dry winters are cool, with temperatures that range from 25° to 32° Fahrenheit (–4° to 0° Celsius). Summers are comfortably warm and have a temperature range of 64° to 73° F (18° to 23° C).

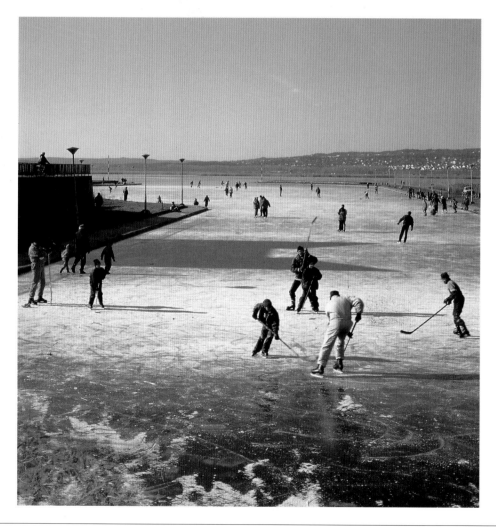

Left:
At times, Hungary can have unusually cold winters, and temperatures have dropped as low as –29° F (–34° C).

Plants and Animals

Only about 18 percent of Hungary's land still has forests. The rest is either pasture land or has been cleared for farming. Forests are mainly beech, oak, lime, and other **deciduous** trees.

The wildlife of Hungary's forests includes deer, wild pigs, foxes, and rodents, and Hortobágy National Park has some of the largest birds in Europe. Aggtelek National Park has Ural owls and other birds rarely seen in Hungary.

Above: Many of the beech forests in Hungary are being cut down for use in industries.

Below: Storks (*below*), as well as cranes, ducks, and herons, are among Hungary's native birds.

History

Until the end of the fourth century, the area that is now Hungary was part of the Roman Empire. Over the next four centuries, it was taken over by, first, Germanic tribes, then Slavs, and, later, the **nomadic** Avars. Around 800, after Charlemagne had defeated the Avars, Hungary became part of Europe's Carolingian empire.

In 892, the Carolingian emperor, Arnulf, asked the Magyars to help him defend his empire. Instead, the

Above:
The Magyars are believed to have come to Hungary from southwestern Russia, near the Ural Mountains.

Left: The Museum of Aquincum, in Budapest, over-looks the ruins of the ancient Roman city of Aquincum.

Magyars, led by Árpád, fought against Arnulf and, by 907, had conquered the land known as Hungary. Árpád's great-great-grandson, Stephen I, became the first king of Hungary in 1000.

Mongols and Turks

In 1241, Hungary was **invaded** by the Mongols. Although they ruled for only one year, they killed about half of the people and badly damaged the country. When the Ottoman Turks invaded, in the 1500s, they divided the country into three regions, each with its own ruler.

The Hapsburg Years

When the Turks were driven out of Hungary, in 1686, Austria's Hapsburg empire took power. Rebellions in 1703 and 1848, however, brought reforms that restored a Hungarian **monarchy**. Although Hungary resisted Austria's attempts to take back full control of the country, a dual Austro-Hungarian monarchy was established in 1867. This government gave Hungary full independence, except in matters of defense, finance, and foreign affairs.

Above:
This castle in Fertőd belonged to the Esterházy family. This family gained its wealth and power by supporting the Hapsburg rulers.

Left:
Emperor Charles I (1887–1922) was the last Hapsburg ruler of Austria.

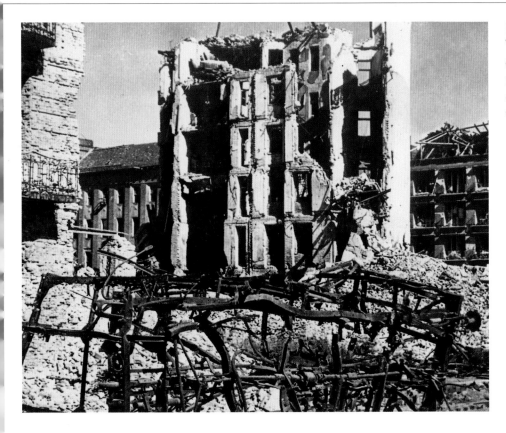

World Wars

During World War I (1914–1918), Hungarians fought alongside the Germans. After the war, the Austro-Hungarian monarchy ended, and more than half of Hungary's land was given to neighboring countries.

Although Hungarians wanted to be **neutral** in World War II, the Germans forced them to fight against the Allies, and Hungary lost more land.

Communism

In November 1945, some winners in Hungary's first free elections were **communists**. With support from the former Soviet Union, Hungary soon became a one-party, communist state. Disliking communism, Hungarians revolted in 1956, but Soviet troops brutally crushed the uprising. Hungary remained a communist state until 1989.

Left:
To symbolize the end of communism in 1989, soldiers cut the barbed wire that had defined Hungary's borders.

King Matthias Corvinus (1443–1490)

Matthias I was a kind ruler and a good soldier. He defended Hungary against the Turks and made the country a European center of art, culture, and politics.

King Matthias Corvinus

Empress Maria Theresa (1717–1780)

Because her father, Hapsburg king Charles III, had no male successors, Maria Theresa became Hungary's first female ruler, in 1740.

Empress Maria Theresa

Lajos Kossuth (1802–1894)

After the 1848 rebellion, Lajos Kossuth quickly drew up the April Laws, greatly reducing Hapsburg control in Hungary. Kossuth fled the country in 1849, but the April Laws became the foundation of the Austro-Hungarian monarchy.

Lajos Kossuth

Government and the Economy

A **parliament** known as the National Assembly, or Országgyülés, is the main unit of government in Hungary. It has 386 members, who are elected by the people. All Hungarians over the age of eighteen may vote. Members of the parliament elect Hungary's president, and the leader of the party that has the most members is the prime minister.

Above: Hungary's large and luxurious parliament building has twenty-nine staircases.

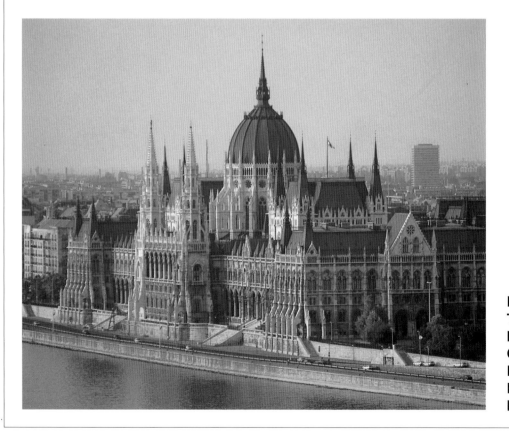

Left: The building that houses Hungary's Országgyülés is in Budapest. It is the largest parliament building in Europe.

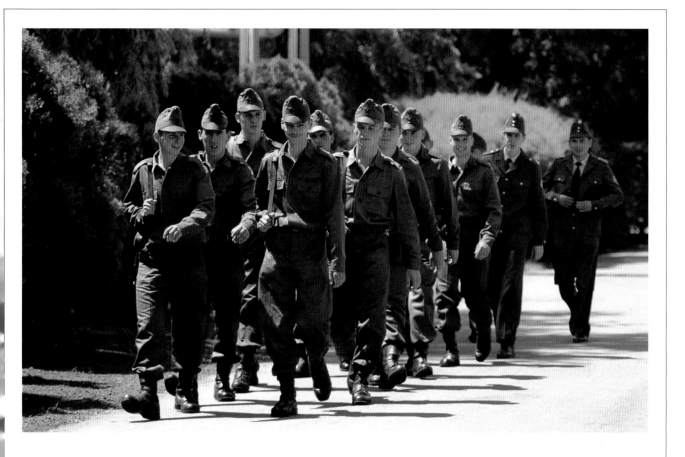

Local Government

On local levels, Hungary's government consists of nineteen county councils, in **rural** areas, twenty municipal county councils, in **urban** areas, as well as the Metropolitan Council of Budapest, which serves the country's capital city. All of these councils are divided into smaller councils. Local governments in Hungary are responsible for health, education, and transportation matters.

Above:
In 2000, about two million Hungarians belonged to the country's military forces. Hungarian males over age eighteen must each serve about a year of military service.

Economy

After the fall of communism in 1989, Hungary developed a **free-market economy**. The government encourages the growth of private businesses and tries to provide benefits for small- and medium-sized companies.

Only about 5 percent of Hungary's economy comes from agriculture. The country's farmers grow a variety of fruits and vegetables, including wheat, corn, rice, apples, and plums.

Above:
The villagers of Tokaj grow a special type of grape used to make a popular wine called Aszú.

Left: In addition to raising fruits and vegetables, Hungarian farmers raise cattle and many types of poultry, such as geese.

Above:
This coal mine and the town around it are reminders of how important the mining industry was to Hungary's economy in the communist years.

Natural Resources

Mining and metals have been important industries for Hungary's economy since the communist years. The country has large amounts of mercury, uranium, lead, **dolomite**, and **bauxite**.

Manufacturing

Most of the products Hungary **exports** are manufactured. They include paper, automobiles, construction materials, medicines, and processed foods. About 30 percent of the country's workforce have jobs in manufacturing.

People and Lifestyle

Nearly 90 percent of Hungary's ten million people are descendants of the Magyars. The rest are Romanies, or Gypsies, and Germans, with small numbers of Serbs, Romanians, and Slovaks. Over the course of Hungary's turbulent history, about five million Hungarians have **migrated** to other countries, including the United States.

Below: Families in Hungary are smaller today than before World War I. Most young Hungarians are choosing to have fewer children than their parents or grandparents had.

Left:
Although thought of as wanderers, most of Hungary's Romanies have permanent homes in villages or near cities. This colorful culture is known all over the world, yet Romanies often face discrimination, especially related to education and employment.

Minority Groups

At about 4 percent of the population, Romanies are the largest minority group in Hungary. About 3 percent of Hungarians are Germans, the second largest minority. To protect minority groups, the government does not allow **discrimination** of any kind, and many of Hungary's laws specifically protect Romanies. Unfortunately, these laws are not always followed.

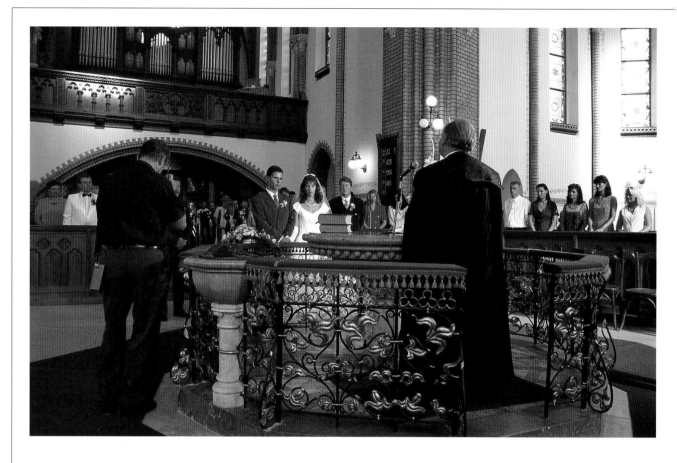

Family Values

Although Hungary's history of war and communism has broken down its traditional structure of large, close-knit families, Hungarians still try to bring many family members together on special occasions, such as Christmas and Easter and even family vacations. Modern Hungarian families usually include just a father, a mother, and their unmarried children.

Above:
Despite decades of communist interference in their religious heritage, most Hungarians still have a church ceremony when they get married.

Women in Hungary

Traditionally, men were the heads of Hungarian households. They worked on farms or in factories, while women stayed at home in their traditional roles as mothers and homemakers.

Since 1989, many Hungarian women have joined the country's workforce. With eight hours a day on the job, plus another four hours of household chores, they now have far less leisure time.

Below:
Today, many Hungarian women, especially those living in the cities, are financially independent.

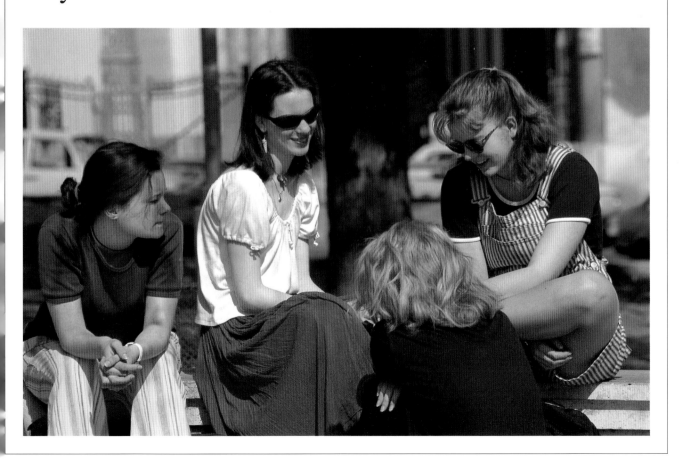

Education

Hungary offers free education, and all children between the ages of six and sixteen must attend school. Elementary school lasts eight years. At age fifteen, most students start secondary, or high, school, which lasts four years. For their secondary education, students can choose to attend a college preparatory school, a technical school, or a school specializing in music or fine arts.

Below: Hungarian parents usually enroll their children who are less than six years old in kindergartens.

Left: The Eger Cathedral, which is located near Eger University, is world famous.

Hungarian students begin higher education in colleges or universities at age nineteen. Not only is higher education free, but some students also receive an allowance to attend. Hungary has eighty schools of higher education. Nineteen are universities. The most respected universities are in Budapest. They include Budapest University of Economic Sciences and Eötvös Loránd University of Sciences.

Religion

Above:
The artistic detail
of Eger Cathedral's
interior design is
a breathtakingly
beautiful sight.

Historically, the Roman Catholic
Church has played a leading role in
Hungarian society and politics. For
many years, however, the country's
communist government discouraged
the practice of religion, often marching
outside churches to disturb services.
Today, Hungary has religious freedom,
and the Roman Catholic Church is still
an important part of Hungarian life.

Almost 70 percent of Hungarians are Roman Catholics, 20 percent are Calvinist Protestants, and 5 percent are members of the Lutheran faith. The rest belong to minority religions such as Judaism.

Jews have lived in Hungary since the time of the Roman Empire, but after World War II and the **Holocaust**, the number dropped dramatically.

Below: The Dohány Street Synagogue, in Budapest, is the largest synagogue in Europe and the second largest in the world. Today, Hungary has over 100,000 Jews.

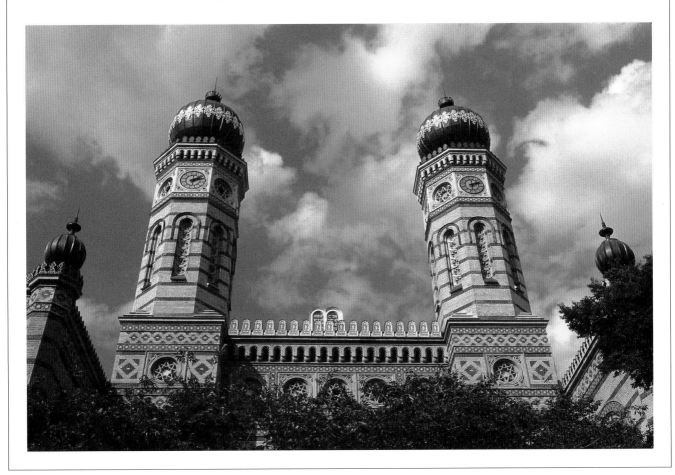

Language

Experts believe that the Hungarian language is one of a group of languages spoken mainly in northeastern Europe and western Siberia. It is very different from other European languages, but has borrowed some words from the Slavic, Latin, German, and Turkish languages. Unique sounds in, for example, words such as *szálloda* (SAH-low-daw) and *rendörség* (REN-duhr-shage), which mean "hotel" and "police," are usually not recognizable to English speakers.

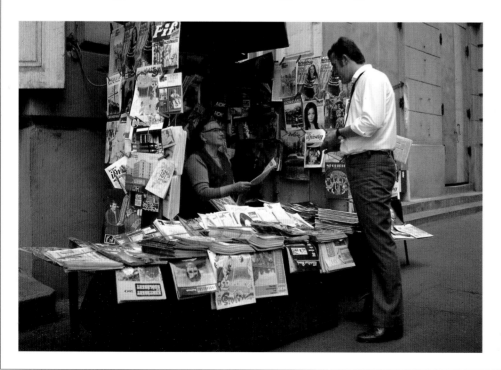

Left: A variety of newspapers and magazines are sold at newsstands on Hungary's streets.

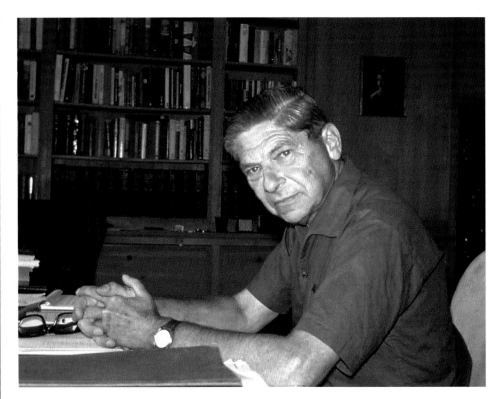

Literature

Early Hungarian writings were mainly
religious works translated from Latin,
but nonreligious literature flourished
in the 1700s. Famous writers at that
time included Benedek Komjáti, Gábor
Pesti, and János Sylvester. Productivity
slowed down in the 1800s and 1900s
as the Turkish invasion, the Hapsburgs,
World Wars, German occupation, and
communism smothered the creativity
of Hungarian writers.

Arts

Music

Hungary is the homeland of many well-known composers of classical music. *Hungarian Rhapsody No. 2*, composed by Franz Liszt (1811–1886), is still heard today. Piano pieces written by composer Béla Bartók (1881–1945) captured and preserved the folk music of Hungary and neighboring countries.

Below: The music of the Romanies is part of Hungary's folk-music tradition. Like Béla Bartók, composer Zoltán Kodály (1882–1967) tried to preserve the folk music of his homeland.

Dance

When the Magyars settled in Hungary, they brought their dances with them. Considered **pagan** customs, these ancient dances were banned by the Roman Catholic Church in the tenth century. Since that time, Hungarian dance has been influenced by the music and steps of Italian, German, and Romany dances. The *Csárdás* (CHAHR-dahsh), Hungary's national dance, was developed in the 1800s.

Embroidery

Hungarian **embroidery**, which is done by men as well as women, is a very artistic craft. Designs are mainly small to medium flower patterns in bright, harmonious colors, usually stitched onto soft fabric, such as linen or cotton. The embroidery is then used to make a variety of items ranging from dresses to bedsheets to tablecloths. Hungarian tailors embroider directly onto coats, vests, and cloaks and take pride in their intricate designs. Embroidery designs in Hungary vary from region to region.

Left: Traditional Hungarian lace and embroidery have been combined to create this colorful and decorative tablecloth.

Architecture

Because Budapest has been rebuilt so many times, its architecture reflects the city's history. Today, modern glass and metal structures stand side by side with historical buildings and even ancient ruins. Budapest also has some uniquely Hungarian architecture. Known as Hungarian art nouveau, it blends local folk art with Oriental designs.

Above:
The architecture of the Gresham Palast, a building located near the Chain Bridge in Budapest, is Hungarian art nouveau, a style that developed in the early 1900s.

Leisure

Most Hungarians like to spend their leisure time with family and friends. In the cities, couples often go out together to see a movie or to have dinner at a restaurant. Some of the wealthier city residents own country homes, where friends and family members are invited to spend weekends and holidays.

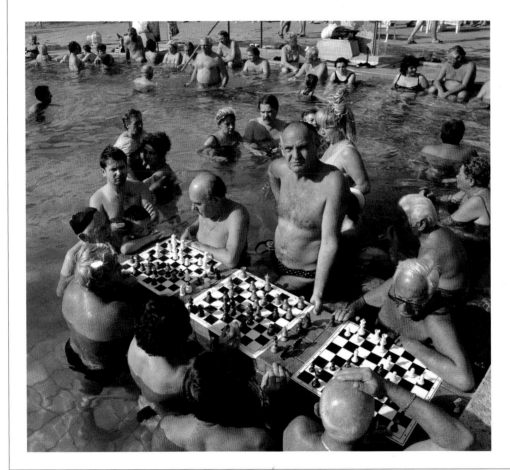

Left: These older Hungarians are enjoying two favorite activities at the same time, playing chess and soaking in spas, or hot springs.

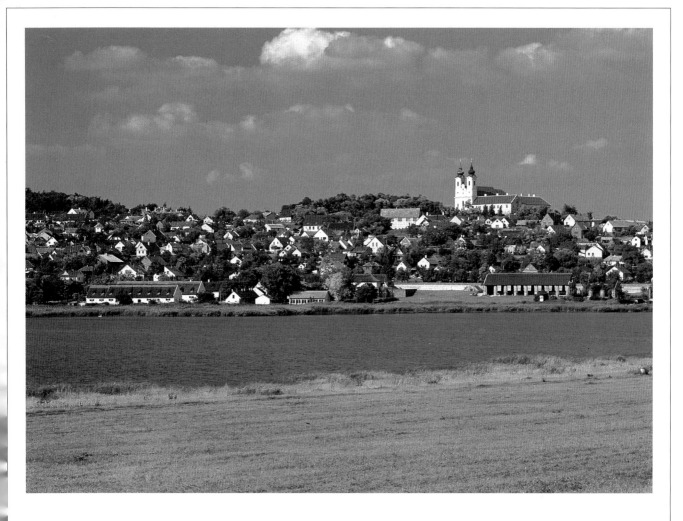

Living in a landlocked country, Hungarians appreciate any chance to be in, on, or near water. Lake Balaton, Hungary's largest single body of water, attracts thousands of local visitors and tourists every year. Activities on the lake include swimming, fishing, and sailing. In the area around the lake, visitors can hike, camp, or visit a zoo!

Above: Beautiful Lake Balaton is 60 miles (97 km) southwest of Budapest.

Sports

Over the years, Hungarians have won many Olympic gold medals. Swimmer Attila Czene won a gold medal in 1996. He also set an Olympic record for the 200-meter men's individual **medley**. At the 2000 Olympics, Hungary won a total of eight gold medals, in canoeing, fencing, gymnastics, water polo, and swimming, as well as six silver medals and three bronze medals.

Above:
Hungarians are enthusiastic soccer fans. The stadiums are filled whenever home teams, such as Ferencváros and Kispest-Honvéd, are playing.

Hungary's national soccer team is known as the "Golden Team." In the 1950s, led by **legendary** soccer star Ferenc Puskás, the team was unbeaten for thirty games. Hungary also won the Olympic gold medal in 1952 and was the first European team to beat England at Wembley Stadium in London.

In recent years, tennis has become very popular in Hungary, especially with the younger and wealthier fans. Both Monica Seles and Martina Hingis are international tennis stars who have Hungarian roots.

Left:
In 1998, tennis star Monica Seles was victorious over Alexandra Fusai of France in the All-England Championships at Wimbledon.

Holidays

Many of the holidays celebrated in Hungary are religious holidays, reflecting the strong position of the Roman Catholic faith in Hungarian life. St. Stephen's Day, on August 20, honors King Stephen I of Árpád, who converted Hungarians to Christianity. The Roman Catholic Church declared Stephen a saint in 1083. Good Friday is another important religious holiday.

Below: Dancing is included in the public celebrations on St. Stephen's Day in the town of Eger.

Christmas is a particularly special holiday in Hungary. Preparations begin on St. Nick's Day (December 6). The night before, children place their shoes near a window, and St. Nick, who is Hungary's Santa Claus, fills clean shoes with candy and dirty shoes with twigs and stones. Christmas eve starts with a feast. Then children stay out of sight while their parents decorate the Christmas tree. After opening gifts, the family attends a midnight Mass.

Food

Hungarians have a proud tradition of making hearty meals out of simple foods and inexpensive meats. Goulash is the best known Hungarian dish. It was originally the food of herdsmen on the Hungarian plains. Traditional goulash contained small pieces of meat mixed with onions and seasoned with **paprika**. Today, it includes vegetables such as carrots and potatoes.

Below:
Paprika and garlic are so commonly used in Hungarian dishes that some shops in Hungary sell only these two items.

Breakfast in Hungary is a simple meal of fresh bread and a hot drink. Lunch usually starts with a clear soup. One popular soup is made of tomatoes and fish. A typical dinner will include spicy sausages, cheese, and bread.

Hungarians like to end their meals with desserts. Dobos torte is a famous Hungarian dessert created in 1885 by a pastry chef named József Dobos. It is six thin layers of sponge cake with creamy **mocha** filling and topped with a caramel glaze.

A B C D

International
Boundary

County
Boundary

■ Capital

● City

River

1

CZECH
REPUBLIC

SLOVAKIA

Carpathian

Aggtelek
National Park

2

AUSTRIA

Danube

Northern Mountain
Mount Kékes
(3,327ft/1,014m)▲

● Ege

N

●Fertőd

LITTLE ALFÖLD

BUDAPEST
■
BUDAPEST

Tis

3

Bakony Mountains

Danube

GREAT ALFÖI

Lake
Balaton

SLOVENIA

4

CROATIA

SERBIA

5

Danube

HUNGARY

42

E   **F**

UKRAINE

●Tokaj

rtobágy
tional Park

ROMANIA

Aggtelek National
   Park D2
Austria B2–A4

Bakony Mountains
   B3–C3
Budapest (city) C3
Budapest
   (county) C3

Carpathian
   Mountains
   B1–F1
Croatia A4–C5
Czech Republic
   A1–C1

Danube River
   A2–D5

Eger D2

Fertőd B3

Great Alföld D3–D4

Hortobágy National
   Park E3

Lake Balaton
   B4–C3
Little Alföld B3–C3

Mount Kékes D2

Northern
   Mountains D2

Romania E3–F5

Serbia C4–E5
Slovakia B2–F1
Slovenia A3–A5

Tisza River D5–F2
Tokaj E2

Ukraine F1–F2

Quick Facts

Official Name   Republic of Hungary

Capital   Budapest

Official Language   Hungarian

Population   10,106,017 (July 2001 estimate)

Land Area   35,919 square miles (93,030 square km)

Highest Point   Mount Kékes 3,327 feet (1,014 m)

Border Countries   Austria, Croatia, Romania, Serbia, Slovakia, Slovenia, Ukraine

Major Rivers   Danube, Tisza

Major Religions   Roman Catholic, Calvinist Protestant, Lutheran

Holidays   National Day (March 15)
Good Friday (March/April)
Saint Stephen's Day (August 20)
Saint Nick's Day (December 6)
Christmas Day (December 25)

Currency   Hungarian Forint (HUF 248 = U.S. $1 in 2002)

Opposite: A colorful, patterned roof is a distinctive feature of Matthias Church in Budapest.

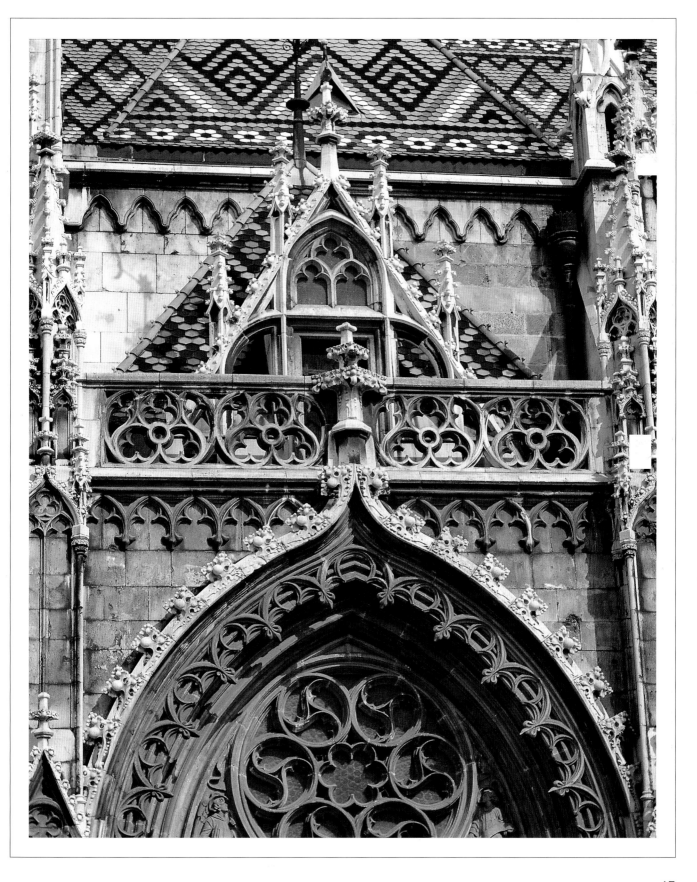

Glossary

arc: a curved line.

bauxite: the mineral from which aluminum is made.

communists: people who support a political system in which the government owns and controls all goods and resources.

deciduous: losing or shedding leaves each year.

discrimination: the practice of treating a person or group unfairly because of differences such as race or religion.

dolomite: a mineral that is the main source of magnesium in Earth's crust.

embroidery: the art of decorating fabric by hand-stitching colorful designs on it with a needle and thread.

exports (v): sells to other countries.

free-market economy: a system of producing and trading goods with little government control and prices that are normally determined by supply and demand.

Holocaust: the mass killing of European Jews by Nazis during World War II.

invaded: entered by force, usually by an enemy seeking to conquer or control.

landlocked: surrounded entirely by land.

legendary: historically famous for having outstanding abilities.

medley: a relay race in swimming in which each team member uses a different stroke.

migrated: moved permanently.

mocha: a chocolaty coffee flavor.

monarchy: a system of government controlled by a king or a queen.

neutral: not supporting either side in a dispute such as a war.

nomadic: moving from place to place with no permanent home.

pagan: based on material and physical pleasure without any religious or moral foundation.

paprika: a red cooking spice made of dried, finely ground sweet peppers.

parliament: a unit of government that makes laws.

plateaus: wide areas of high, flat land.

rural: related to the countryside.

tribes: distinct groups or divisions of people belonging to the same family, nation, or race.

urban: related to cities and large towns.

More Books to Read

Cooking the Hungarian Way. Easy Menu Ethnic Cookbooks series. Magdolna Hargittai (Lerner)

Eastern Europe. Country Fact Files series. Patrick Burke (Raintree/Steck-Vaughn)

Gypsies. Endangered Cultures series. Elizabeth Sirimarco (Smart Apple Media)

Hanna's Cold Winter. Trish Marx (Lerner)

Hungary. Modern Nations of the World series. Anne Ake (Lucent Books)

Hungary … in Pictures. Visual Geography series. Lerner Department of Geography (Lerner)

Martina Hingis. Sports Superstars series. Richard Rambeck (Child's World)

Monica Seles. Making Their Mark series. Liza N. Burby (Powerkids Press)

One-Time Dog Market at Buda and Other Hungarian Folktales. Irma Molnar, translator (Linnet Books)

Videos

Budapest. Super Cities series. (International Video Network)

Hungarian Rhapsody. (New Vision Video)

Hungary: Land of Hospitality. Video Visits series. (International Video Network)

Village Life and Music in Hungary. (Sussex Video Ltd.)

Web Sites

www.bajabela.sulinet.hu/tubi/iearn/ tales/tales.htm

www.castles.org/castles/Europe/ Central_Europe/Hungary/

www.fsz.bme.hu/hungary/budapest/ kepek/szines.htm

www.zuzu.org/hung.html

Due to the dynamic nature of the Internet, some web sites stay current longer than others. To find additional web sites, use a reliable search engine with one or more of the following keywords to help you locate information about Hungary. Keywords: *Budapest,* Csárdás, *Danube, Eger, goulash, Hapsburg, Lake Balaton, Magyars.*

Index